The Friendship Pact

Other APPLE® PAPERBACKS by Susan Beth Pfeffer:

Kid Power
Starting with Melodie
Truth or Dare

Coming Soon:
Kid Power Strikes Back

The Friendship Pact

Susan Beth Pfeffer

AN
APPLE®
PAPERBACK

SCHOLASTIC INC.
New York Toronto London Auckland Sydney

ISBN 0-590-32143-9

12 11 10 9 8 7 6 5 4 3 6 7 8 9/8 0 1/9

Printed in the U.S.A. 28

To Marilyn Marlow for her endless patience.

1

For the past two years, I have been hopelessly, completely in love with Rabbit O'Shea. And for all my life, I have hated to sew.

As far as love goes, I'm also every bit as much in love with Ross Perlman. And up until last Friday, I wasn't sure which one I loved more.

Of course all the pictures I have up on my walls of Rabbit are pictures of Ross, too, since Rabbit's the character Ross plays on *Joyride*, my favorite TV show. Only Ross really isn't anything like Rabbit, so I have lots of pictures of just him on my walls. Ross, after all, went to Dartmouth, which is the only thing my father likes about him. Not that they ever met. But Dad went to Dartmouth, too. He didn't like it very much, but he has a sentimental feeling about other people who went there. Anyway, I didn't love Ross because he went to Dartmouth, although I admit it gave me a little thrill to realize he went there and not to Harvard or Yale. The thought that Ross was in the same buildings, the same dorms, maybe even the same room as my father, made me feel almost as though I knew him.

But I loved Rabbit, too, and Rabbit never went anywhere to college. My father hates Rabbit. As a matter of fact, every time *Joyride* is on the air, my father leaves the room, after saying all kinds of insulting things about it. I just let him talk. I love *Joyride*. It's my absolute favorite show in the whole world, because of Rabbit. He's sort of the main character. There are other characters who are very important, but nothing would happen on the show if it wasn't for Rabbit. Rabbit talks tough and he gets into trouble a lot, but he always straightens things out. That's how his character got his nickname; Rabbit is always hopping in and out of jams. And lots of times, Rabbit gets a chance to sing, too. That's practically my favorite part of the show, when Rabbit gets to sing. But basically *Joyride* is a comedy, and I always laugh when I watch it. So does Scott, my brother. He's fifteen (I'm twelve), and he says *Joyride* is just for kids, and he can't understand why I love Rabbit so much, but he watches it, too. So does my mother. Whenever Dad acts like he's mad that Mom watches it, she just shrugs her shoulders and says, "I can't help it. Rabbit's kind of cute." And that from a mother.

My best friend Andrea Todd and I were sitting in homeroom a few weeks ago when Caroline Earle came in and sat down with a flounce. Caroline does everything with a flounce, and she doesn't even care when the boys make fun of her, which they do all the time. I don't blame them. Caroline acts like she's royalty. That's because her father is mayor and her mother is this big shot who plans every cultural event that takes place in our town. We have about eight cultural events a year — concerts or plays that are on tour — so eight times a year Mrs. Earle is a real big shot, and all year round Mr. Earle is. And that's why Caroline flounces.

This time she flounced with more excitement than usual. "I have something fabulous to tell you," she whispered in my general vicinity.

Caroline likes me. I don't have the slightest idea why, since she must know I don't really like her. She's my friend, though. We've been friends since kindergarten, she and Andrea and Mary Kate Donahue and I, and I haven't liked her all that time. Caroline doesn't seem to care.

"What?" I asked. Caroline always has something fabulous to tell me. Usually it's about some dumb law her father signed, or some big present her parents bought her. My mother, who doesn't like Caroline either, says she's spoiled rotten.

"Rabbit is coming here to give a concert!" she whispered, loud enough for me and Andrea to hear her.

I nearly fainted. "Not *the* Rabbit?" I said, trying to sound cool. "Not Ross Perlman?"

"What other Rabbit is there?" Caroline said. "He's going to give a concert right here, in our auditorium."

Our school has the biggest auditorium in town, so all of Mrs. Earle's cultural events take place here. Still, Rabbit didn't exactly seem like the string quartets she usually brings into town. "Did your mother arrange it?" I asked. If Caroline's mother had actually talked to Ross Perlman, I thought I would die.

Caroline shook her head. I guess she didn't much like the question. "No," she admitted. "Mr. Thomas arranged it all. It's a benefit for hemophilia."

Ross Perlman's cousin has hemophilia, so Ross gives benefits for the National Hemophilia Foundation. All the articles said so. They said not only was he multitalented and very cute, but dedicated to eradicating the evil of disease. I made sure my parents gave some money to the National Hemophilia Foundation the year before, without telling them why. I guess they figured I was dedicated to eradicating the evil of disease, too.

Mr. Thomas is very important in the National Hemophilia Foundation, so it was probably no big deal to him to ask Ross Perlman to give a concert here. But it made me feel weak in my knees. I was awfully glad I was sitting down. If I ever fainted because Rabbit was coming to town, the boys would never let me live it down.

"When's the concert?" Andrea asked.

"Three weeks from Friday," Caroline said. "Let's all get tickets together."

"Me, too," Mary Kate said. She sits two rows down, so I could tell Caroline's whisper was traveling pretty well. My mother says Mrs. Earle knows how to make a lot of noise just being quiet, and Caroline's like that, too.

I was about to agree with everybody, when the first wave of my wonderful idea hit me. It wasn't like I thought about it, the way you work out an arithmetic problem. It just struck me, and I practically gasped when I thought of it. Only I couldn't say anything about it until I had a chance to be alone with Andrea.

Everybody loves Rabbit, but nobody loves him quite as much as Andrea and I do. We have to be his two biggest fans in the world. Take the time our movie theater showed a horror movie Ross

Perlman had been in before he got famous playing Rabbit. It was a terrible movie, even though Ross did get to sing two songs in it, but that didn't stop Andrea and me from seeing the movie together four times that week. Andrea's walls would be full of pictures of Ross, except she lives in an apartment and her parents won't let her load the walls with photographs, so she just has four of them on her bulletin board. But they're really good pictures, and she has a scrapbook all about him, too, that she's filled with articles. I would have had one myself, except Andrea thought of it first, and I didn't want to seem like a copycat. Besides, I get to plaster my walls with Rabbit pictures, and I don't want to be greedy. So I help Andrea find articles and we Scotch-tape them in together, and it's almost like the book belongs to both of us.

Andrea and I are in the same homeroom, so we have the same classes, which gives us plenty of time to talk and write notes during the school day. Even so, we have a signal which means, This is so important that we can't talk about it in public; I'll talk to you after school. What we do is cough twice and wink our right eye. I'm not a very good eye-winker, but Andrea always gets the signal.

I had just finished coughing and winking when Mr. Carpenter, our homeroom teacher, came in, and we had to stand up and say the pledge of allegiance instead. At first I was glad I had the whole day in front of me, because I still felt flattened from the wave of my idea, and wanted a chance to think about it before I let Andrea know.

By lunch, it seemed half the school knew about Rabbit, and the cafeteria was buzzing. Andrea, Mary Kate, Caroline, and I did our share of buzzing. We discussed exactly what we'd wear and whether we should bring our Ross Perlman albums to the concert and hold them high over our heads so he'd know he had fans there. Caroline said she'd do that but she was absolutely not going to squeal. I made a bet with her right then and there that she'd squeal just like the rest of us. Caroline might be pretty obnoxious, but she loves Rabbit, too. She doesn't have any pictures of him hanging in her bedroom because her parents won't let her, but she has a huge color picture of him plastered on the front of her looseleaf notebook.

I didn't pay very much attention to anything else at school that day. I'm a pretty good student, and I don't daydream very much, but my mind was on Ross Perlman and how he was going to walk through the same halls I walk through. It was like Dartmouth, only a thousand times better, because he'd be breathing the very same air I do, and not just whatever air was left over at Dartmouth from when my father was there. I wasn't alone daydreaming. Two of my teachers complained that none of the kids paid any attention to anything they were saying all day. My science teacher even threatened to give us a test on rabbits, right then and there, since that was all we were thinking about.

By last period I was dying for school to be over, so I could tell Andrea my wonderful idea. Last period is home ec, which is my least favorite class, anyway. We have it every Monday, Wednesday, and Friday, while the boys have shop. That's just for the first half of the year. Then we have shop and the boys have home ec. On Tuesdays and Thursdays we have art together, which is better. In home ec all you learn how to do is cook and sew. Cooking isn't too bad. We learned how to make cookies, and French toast, and pizza. All pizza was, was white bread with cheese and ketchup on it warmed up together. Real pizza is a lot better.

But cooking was a thousand times better than sewing, which is what we'd been doing lately. It isn't like I'm weird for hating to sew. Everybody in my family does, so we never do any. Mom has this arrangement with her friend Mrs. Katz, that every time something needs sewing, Mrs. Katz does it for her, and every time Mrs. Katz needs something baked, Mom does it. Mom says it balances out in the end.

Miss Collins, our home ec teacher, loves sewing, though. I think if she had to choose between sewing and eating, she'd pick sewing. Of course if all she knows how to make are cookies and French toast and white-bread pizza, I don't blame her.

"Girls, I have an assignment for you," she announced after looking at the hems we were sewing. She frowned when she looked at mine. She always does. My mother says it's miracle enough any child of hers can thread a needle, and doesn't mind at all that my hems run diagonally.

We all groaned when she said "assignment." Home ec doesn't have homework like the rest of our classes, but those assignments could drive you crazy.

"It's going to be due two weeks from Friday," Miss Collins said. "So write it down in your assignment books now. I won't be reminding you of it every day, you know."

We all took out our assignment books and prepared to take notes.

"Each one of you will be expected to make an apron," Miss Collins said, then paused dramatically.

None of us said anything. I might have sighed, but Mrs. Collins didn't notice.

"I want each of you to go out and buy two yards of cotton," Miss Collins instructed us. "Any color you want. A print, even, if you feel like it. The only instructions I have about the apron are that it be hemmed, have at least one pocket, and, of course, sashes to tie around your back. Naturally I hope you'll apply your imaginations and make your aprons more decorative than that."

Caroline murmured agreement. Caroline does needlepoint.

"Originality will be a factor in grading," Miss Collins continued. "But I'll give a good grade to a simple apron well-made. Three weeks should give you more than enough time to make up a design and execute it. And, of course, after I've graded them, I'll give you your aprons back, and you'll be able to use them when you cook."

I looked down at my assignment book and realized that instead of taking notes about the apron, I'd been doodling pictures of rabbits. It didn't matter. I could write notes about aprons for the rest of my life, and I'd still be lucky to make one come out in one piece.

Just when I gave up hope that the bell would ever ring it did. We all jumped out of our chairs, but it was only the warning bell, so we spent the next five minutes putting the needles and thread away and straightening out our school things. Miss

Collins came up to me while I was returning the thread.

"I expect you to work extra hard on your apron, Tracy," she said to me. "Frankly, I'm surprised a girl as smart as you does so poorly in sewing."

I thought about explaining about heredity, but it didn't seem worth it. "I try," I said, which was true enough. I do try. Not very hard, maybe, but still I try.

"Then I think you'll have to try just a bit harder," Miss Collins said. "I want you to make an apron we'll both be proud of. Do you think you can do that?"

I nodded because I had to. There was no way I could make a decent apron. I knew my limitations.

Miss Collins probably would have told me even more about the apron she expected me to make, except that the final bell rang and I seized my chance to escape. Andrea and I ran out of the room as fast as we could, so we'd beat Caroline and Mary Kate to our lockers, and get a head start. We beat them by a clear five seconds, and before they had the chance to say anything to us, we were out of the hallway and halfway down the front steps.

Andrea began running toward my house, so I ran to keep up with her. We got home in record time, but we were so winded we couldn't talk for a moment. Instead, we threw our books on the living room sofa and collapsed on the floor next to it.

"Andrea," I said, still huffing.

"What?" she panted.

"What's the most important thing that's ever happened in our lives?" I asked her.

"Rabbit's coming to town," she said.

"Right," I said, and I felt as excited by my wonderful wave of an idea as I had when it first hit me. "But just having him here isn't important enough. Andrea, we just have to meet him!"

2

"Tracy, you are totally and completely insane," Andrea said. "How can we possibly meet him? They'll probably guard him with every policeman in this town."

"There's got to be a way," I said. "We just have to think of one."

Andrea was silent for a moment. "What would we say to him?" she asked finally.

"We'll worry about that when we meet him," I said. "You're willing to try?"

Andrea nodded. "I'll try. But let's make an unbreakable pact that if one of us gets to meet him, so does the other one."

Andrea liked unbreakable pacts, but this one I was more than willing to agree to. For all my determination to meet Ross Perlman, I'd never know what to say to him if I was alone. My mouth would probably just drop open and stay that way.

"I agree to this pact," I said, just the way Andrea liked.

"And let's not tell anybody else about our pact," Andrea said. "If we tell people we're going to meet him, they'll want to join us."

"More likely they'd just laugh at us," I said.

"Either way, let's keep it to ourselves. We don't want Mary Kate to interfere. Or Caroline. Especially Caroline."

"You're right," I said. "Caroline would probably want to sew him an apron. We'll keep it to ourselves."

"Great," Andrea said. "But how can we meet him?"

We were instantly silent. It's one thing to decide to meet someone; it's quite another to figure out a way. "Maybe he'll get a flat tire right in front of your house," Andrea said doubtfully. "Then you could keep him here and call me."

"What should we do, strew the streets with thumbtacks?" I asked.

"Well. . . ." Andrea said.

"Come on, Andrea, we've got to be practical about this," I said. "Meeting Ross Perlman would be the most important thing that ever happened to us — *ever*. Maybe for the rest of our lives. We can't leave it to chance."

So we were silent again. Then Andrea said,

"Your father's an editor at the paper. Maybe he could help us."

"Dad?" I said. "Dad hates Ross Perlman. He wouldn't help."

"Not even for you?" Andrea said. "His only daughter?"

"Especially not for me," I said. "His only daughter. He thinks the Rabbit's a bad influence."

"How about the reporters?" Andrea suggested. "One of them might be able to help."

"No, I have a better idea," I said. "Uncle Charlie."

"Uncle Charlie?" Andrea said. "I didn't know you had an Uncle Charlie."

"He's an honorary uncle," I said. "He's the managing editor of the paper. He and Dad are old friends, and he comes over here for supper a lot because he's divorced, and Mom worries about him. He has tons of girl friends, and he brings me great presents sometimes, and he always says if I have any problems I should tell him."

"I wish I had an uncle like that," Andrea said.

"This is a problem, right?" I said. "I'll ask him if he can help us meet Ross. After all, Uncle Charlie'll be there. He's almost as important as Caroline's parents."

"I bet he's a lot nicer, too," Andrea said.

"Atilla the Hun is nicer," I said. "But he really

is nice, and I'm sure he'll try to help us. How's that?"

"It's a good start," Andrea said.

"Okay," I said. "You come up with one."

Andrea was silent. "Thumbtacks are a possibility," she said.

"Andrea!" I said. "Come on. Your parents know lots of people."

"Nobody useful," she said.

"Oh yes they do," I said. "Your parents know Mr. Thomas. And he's the one organizing the concert."

"I couldn't ask him," Andrea said. "Mr. Thomas is my father's client. If I went to him, Dad would kill me."

"You've told me what a nice man Mr. Thomas is," I said. "And he's just bound to know Ross. I bet Ross'll be staying at his house, even."

"I don't know," Andrea said. "I'd like to see my thirteenth birthday."

"You're such a coward," I said. "You always expect me to do all the dirty work. Mr. Thomas is bound to know Ross, and he could help us so easily, and you're scared to go to him. Even if he can't help us, he wouldn't tell your father."

"Oh, okay," Andrea said. "But I'll call him myself. It'll make a better impression than if the two of us go charging at him."

"Deal," I said. "I'll ask Uncle Charlie, and you ask Mr. Thomas. Now we need just one more."

"One more?" Andrea said. "We have two already."

"The more chances, the better," I said. "How about your mother? She works at the radio station. Maybe she could help."

"I don't think so," Andrea said. "What would Ross Perlman be doing at our cruddy radio station?"

"Plugging his records?" I asked.

"No," Andrea said. "Remember when the Banjos gave a concert here last year?"

I nodded. The Banjos were a rock group that gave a concert Caroline's mother didn't arrange. It wasn't cultural enough.

"They're nowhere near as big as Ross," Andrea said. "And Mom told me her boss tried to get them to come down to the station, just for a few minutes, even, and they wouldn't. So I don't think Ross will."

"Okay," I said. "What do you suggest, then?"

"I'll buy thumbtacks?" Andrea said.

We were still giggling when Scott came in. He hung his coat up in the hallway closet and put his books down on the dining room table, and then came into the living room.

"If it isn't the Bobbsey twins," he said, and sat

down on the easy chair. "You'd better hang your coats up before Mom gets home."

"I have to be leaving soon, anyway," Andrea said.

"Stay for supper," I said.

"I can't," she said.

"I guess you girls heard," Scott said. "About how the Rabbit's coming to town."

"You know, too?" I asked.

"Sure," Scott said. "The principal at my school announced it over the PA. They were picking girls up off the floor all day."

"We were just daydreaming about meeting him," Andrea said.

"Somebody's going to," Scott said.

"What do you mean?" I asked.

"The contest," Scott said. "Or don't you know about it?"

"What contest?" I asked.

"Lenny's mom picked us up after school," Scott said. "And she had her car radio on to WRAL, and they said they were having a 'Meet the Rabbit Contest.' "

"What do you have to do?" I asked eagerly. "What're the rules?"

"First of all you have to be sixteen or younger," Scott said. "So you certainly qualify for that. If they were doing it on mental age, you'd qualify for six or under, even."

Scott says things like that all the time. Usually I want to kill him, but this time I just kept quiet.

"You have to write an entry in twenty-five words or less about why you want to meet the Rabbit," he said. "And it has to be postmarked by Saturday, because there isn't that much time between now and the concert."

"And the best entry will win?" I asked.

"Sort of," Scott said. "The best five will be put in a hat, and one name'll be selected. The other four will win Rabbit albums."

"Who needs a Rabbit album?" Andrea said. "I have that already."

"Then don't enter the contest," Scott said.

"We have to," I said. "You and me both. Can you enter more than once?"

"Only one shot to a customer," Scott said with a yawn.

"That gives us two chances out of five," I said.

"Assuming we have two of the best entries," Andrea said.

"We will," I said. "We have to. Besides, English is my best subject. Right?"

"Yeah?"

"So I'll write really great entries," I said. "Especially with your help. Want to do it now?"

"I can't," Andrea said. "I have to get home before Mom and Dad do."

"You know what you have to do," I said to her.

"The entry, you mean," she said.

"That, and our project," I said with a cough.

"Oh yeah, our project," she said and coughed right back.

"The two of you sound like you're on your deathbeds," Scott said. "I only wish."

"Aprons," I said, winking at Andrea. "We have to make aprons for home ec. It's our project."

"I guess it'll keep you off the streets," Scott said. "Though you'd have a better chance of getting run over there."

"Oh, Scott," Andrea said, and got her jacket and books. "Don't forget to start sewing, Tracy."

"I won't," I said, trying hard not to giggle. I walked her to the door. "Have your thread?" I blurted out as she started to leave.

"I sure do," she said. "Don't forget the needles and pins."

"How could I?" I said. "We have to sew us up a rabbit."

3

All I wanted to talk about at supper was Rabbit, but I didn't dare. Scott mentioned something about the concert, and Dad made his usual comment about a Dartmouth man gone bad, so I kept my mouth shut.

I had homework due the next day, but not that much, so I decided I'd write my contest entry that night and get it over with. I had just sat down on the living room floor — I do all my best thinking there — when the telephone rang.

"It's for you," Mom called to me. "It's Andrea."

"Andrea," Scott grumbled. "Tracy sees Andrea all day at school and Andrea is always over here visiting and as soon as she gets home, she has this compulsive need to call."

"Oh, shut up," I said, and went to get the phone.

"Don't hog the line," he said to me.

I made a face at him, then picked up the phone. "Hi, Andrea," I said. "Finish your entry yet?"

"That's why I'm calling," she said. "I can't enter."

"What do you mean, you can't enter?" I said. "Of course you can."

"No, I can't," she said. "The contest isn't open to relatives of people who work at the radio station. And that lets me out."

"Oh," I said. That made sense. I could never enter contests the paper held because of Dad.

"You're just going to have to win the contest for both of us," she said. "Tracy, I'm really sorry."

"It's not your fault," I said. "I don't suppose your mother would quit. . . . No, there's no point even asking."

"I already have," Andrea said. "Mom said that would be carrying permissiveness to new heights. Or depths. She couldn't decide which."

"I'll ask Scott if he'll enter for us," I said. "He's under sixteen."

"That's a great idea," Andrea said. "Let me know what happens, and bring your entry in to school tomorrow. I'm dying to read it."

"Sure," I said. "See you then."

" 'Bye," she said, and we hung up. I walked back to the living room, and passed through the dining room on my way. Scott was sitting at the table, doing his geometry, so I figured he wouldn't mind an interruption.

"Hey, Scott," I said as casually as I could. "Want to do me a favor?"

"No," Scott said.

"Come on, it's not a big favor. Just a little one," I said.

"Not even a little one," he said.

"All I want is to use your name," I said. "Andrea can't enter the radio contest to meet the Rabbit, because her mother works there. And we had really counted on having two entries."

"You want me to enter for Andrea?" Scott asked. "You're crazier than I ever thought you were."

"But why?"

"First of all, what if I won? You want me to go to school with everybody thinking I wanted to meet that creep? And if I did win, which one of you would pretend to be Scott Newfield? You or Andrea? Neither one of you is what I'd call sexy, but you're still definitely girls."

"You could take us with you," I said.

"Thanks, but no thanks," he said. "If you're going to win, you'll have to do it on your own."

"Thanks, pal," I said. "Just wait until you want a favor from me."

"I know one favor you can do for me," Scott said. "You can drop dead."

"You first," I said. "Age before beauty."

"Cut it out," Mom said from the kitchen. "Come

on in, Tracy, and tell me exactly what the problem is."

So I went back in and explained to her. She said, "You'll just have to write a great entry and win it on your own. You can do that."

"I can try," I said. "Mom, it means more than anything to me to meet him."

"I can understand," Mom said. "When I was your age, I would have given anything to meet Marlon Brando."

"Marlon Brando?" I said. "But he's so fat."

"Now, maybe, but oh then. . . ." Mom said with a sigh. "Besides, who knows what Ross Perlman's going to look like thirty years from now."

"He'll never be fat," I said. "Do you think I should mention that in my entry?"

"Not if you only have twenty-five words to play with," Mom said. "You know who should help you? Your father. He's used to getting a lot of meaning into very few words."

"I couldn't ask him," I said. "He hates Rabbit."

"Tell him it's for the honor of Dartmouth," Mom said, so I ran to the den and dragged Dad out of it and into the kitchen. By this time Scott had come in, also.

"Good," Mom said. "A family project. *Woman's Day* would be so proud of us."

"Twenty-five words, huh," Dad grumbled. "And the first seven have to be 'I want to meet Ross Perlman because'?"

"No, they don't count," Scott said. "How about 'I want to meet Ross Perlman because I'm crazy'? At least it's honest."

"Any more entries like that and it's back to geometry for you," Mom said. "This is important to Tracy, and I think we should help her. After all, just think how different my life might have been if I'd met Brando."

"Brando?" Dad asked. "How did he come into this?"

"Mom had a crush on him," I said.

"Brando?" Dad said. "No wonder you dragged me to *The Godfather* three times."

"Who did you have a crush on, Dad?" I asked.

"Men don't get crushes," Scott said.

"They sure do," Dad said. "When I was a teenager, I would have given my right arm to meet Debbie Reynolds."

"Debbie Reynolds?" Mom said. "Little wholesome Debbie?"

"I'm a sucker for freckles," Dad said. "Besides, you're hardly one to talk. Brando?"

"I love the torn T-shirt look," Mom replied.

"How about 'I want to meet Ross Perlman because my father loved Debbie Reynolds and my mother loved Marlon Brando and I love Ross Perlman'?" I suggested.

Dad thought about that for a moment. At least I assume that's what he thought about. His mind could have still been on Debbie Reynolds' freckles. "That's not a bad approach," he said. "But the language is a little rough."

"I don't think you have to name the people we had crushes on," Mom said. "I don't mind for myself. Brando, after all, is a great actor. But I'm not sure I want it known all over town that my husband has been crazy for Debbie Reynolds all these years."

"How about something like 'My parents never got to meet the people they had crushes on, and their lives have been in ruins as a result'?" Scott said.

"You'll be a ruin in a minute," Mom said.

"How about 'I want to meet Ross Perlman because my parents never met the people they had crushes on, and I want to break a family tradition'?" I said.

"That's not bad at all," Dad said. "How many words is that?"

We all counted it in our heads and shouted, "Eighteen!" except for Scott, who shouted,

"Twenty!" The reason he hates geometry is because he's so lousy at math.

"I like that a lot," Mom said. "It has a little bit of humor to it, and it's true, and Tracy wrote it herself. It doesn't sound like her parents made it up for her."

"Besides, it doesn't mention Marlon Brando," Dad said. "If I knew you liked men chubby, I wouldn't have been so careful about my weight."

"On the screen I like them chubby," Mom said. "In real life I like them just like you."

"Slightly chubby," Scott muttered. I giggled. Dad does have a belly.

"Of course, it doesn't mention Andrea," I said.

"Why should it?" Scott asked. "She isn't a member of this family yet."

"We made a solemn vow that if one of us got to meet the Rabbit, she'd bring the other one along," I said. "Maybe I should put that in."

"I don't think it's necessary," Dad said. "Besides, are you sure they'll let you bring a friend along if you win?"

"They'll have to," I said. "Otherwise I won't go."

"If it isn't Saint Tracy," Scott said. "You'll go and you know it."

"I think we're creating a problem," Mom said.

"Besides, I'm sure they'll let you bring someone along. Assuming you win."

"I've got to," I said. I knew better than to mention our backup plans for meeting Ross.

"I suggest, then, that you write your entry neatly and get it ready to mail tomorrow," Mom said. "And maybe you'll be lucky and win."

"I hope so," I said, and closed my eyes. "Could you imagine if I actually got to meet him? To shake his hand? Just to say hello?"

"I don't know what all this fuss is about," Dad said, "After all, he's just a — "

"Dartmouth man," Scott and I said along with him.

"I'm going to go to Princeton, myself," Scott said. "Higher class of people there."

"You won't meet any class of people unless you start working on your homework," Mom said. "You, too, Tracy. Write your entry and then get to your schoolwork."

"Okay," I said. First I got a postcard, the way the radio said I should, and I printed my entry neatly on it, then wrote my name, address, phone number, and age on it, so it was pretty crowded, but still neat. Then I sneaked into my parents' bedroom and called Andrea to read her the entry. It was her entry, too, after all. She said it was fine by her, although she couldn't imagine her parents having crushes on anybody, not even Debbie Reynolds. I knew what she meant. It was alarming to learn my mother even thought about things like that.

As I was going through my assignment book to check on how much social studies I was supposed to read that night, I came across the note on the apron. I scowled. Sewing an apron had as much appeal to me then as it had during class. Less than none. But I had almost three weeks to do it in, and how long could it take to put a couple of pieces of material together? I didn't want a masterpiece, after all. I was never going to use it once it was done. Mom and Dad never wore aprons when they cooked, so why should I? And if I ever needed an apron, I could always buy one. It was just a dumb assignment the teacher made up to check and see if we knew how to make hems. As long as Mrs. Katz knew how to make hems, I didn't see any reason to learn.

So I read my social studies and did my arithmetic and English and studied for the science test I had on Wednesday, but in between chapters, lines, problems, and even words, sometimes, I thought about Ross and meeting him and what I'd say and what I'd be wearing and how he'd look at me and what he'd say to me. To Andrea, too, but mostly to me. We'd talk about Dartmouth, and school, and maybe he'd say I should go to Hollywood and try to become an actress. When I was a lot younger, I used to have long, blonde hair and I was always imagining that some Hollywood producer would discover me and have me star in a production of *Alice in Wonderland* , but no one ever did.

I didn't really think Ross Perlman would, either. Just meeting him would be enough, even if neither of us said anything more than hello. That would be enough.

And I'd remember it always, and tell my children about it, the way Mom told me about Marlon Brando. I wondered if maybe Ross could arrange an introduction for her. When I met him, I'd try to remember to ask.

4

That week the only thing we thought about was Rabbit.

I don't think any of us studied for the science test on Wednesday; my science teacher, Mr. Taylor, said he'd never seen a worse set of test papers. We all had Rabbit fever, even the boys. Rabbit's very popular with them, too, even though they don't usually cover their books with Rabbit book covers.

All that week, every time Andrea and I were alone, we talked about Ross and how we were going to meet him. I had entered the radio contest the next morning after writing my entry. I'd kissed the postcard three times for luck, and would have kissed the mailbox, too, except there were other people outside. Besides, I was afraid of germs. So I just crossed my fingers and wished on the brightest star I could find, which was the sun, since it was eight o'clock in the morning.

I felt pretty good about the entry. Andrea said most of the other kids who entered would just write that they wanted to meet Ross Perlman because they loved him. If you eliminated all those, she said, that wouldn't leave much more than five entries, so mine had a real good chance.

Just to be on the safe side, though, we decided to follow through on our original list of people to contact. I figured since I'd gone first, with the entry, Andrea should go first by calling Mr. Thomas, and I told her so. She hemmed and hawed on Tuesday, and Wednesday, but Thursday, during homeroom, she coughed once and winked, which was our signal that she had something to tell me during lunch. So I waited impatiently until then. Maybe Mr. Thomas had said, Certainly, it would be no problem for us to meet him. Ross loved meeting his fans; I'd read that in a magazine called *Meet the Rabbit*, which I bought two copies of — one to read and keep, and one to cut pictures out of for my walls and Andrea's scrapbook. And he certainly didn't have any more devoted fans than Andrea and me. We'd even talked about starting a Ross Perlman Fan Club, except we didn't know how to go about it.

So I doodled all through my morning subjects, yawned when Mr. Taylor complained about how bad our test scores were, and dreamed of talking to Ross. I was absolutely going to mention Marlon Brando to him. Mom was being really nice about how much I wanted to meet Ross, so I figured it was the least I could do.

Andrea and I got on line together at the cafeteria, making sure we were a safe distance from Caroline and Mary Kate. With the noise level in the cafeteria, we didn't have to be too far away to be sure they couldn't hear us.

"You spoke to Mr. Thomas?" I asked eagerly, grabbing a plate of macaroni and cheese.

Andrea took a plate, too. "I called him last night," she said. We both took apples.

"Don't keep me in suspense," I said. "What did he say?"

"He was really nice about it," Andrea said. "But he said he couldn't help us."

"He couldn't!" I cried, loud enough so that at least five kids heard and turned their heads toward us. I blushed. "Why not?" I whispered.

Andrea looked carefully at the milk cartons before picking one. "He said he was really sorry about it," she said. "But he'd promised you-know-who that he wouldn't bother him with people."

"Does that mean 'you-know-who' doesn't want to meet anybody while he's here?" I asked. "Not even the radio contest winner?"

"Shush," Andrea said. "Do you want everybody to know?"

"No," I whispered. "But does it?"

"I don't know," she said. "Mr. Thomas didn't know. He just said he couldn't help. I didn't talk with him for more than a minute."

"Oh," I said, and sighed. "I guess we can't expect all our ideas to turn out winners."

We took our trays to our table, and set them down before Mary Kate and Caroline arrived.

"When are you going to talk to Uncle Charlie?" Andrea asked.

"I figured I'd go over to the paper one day after school," I said. "And ask him at his office."

"Today?"

"No, not today," I said. "One day next week. We still have time."

"Let's not waste the time we have," Andrea said.

"Waste what time?" Caroline asked, as she joined us at the table.

"The time we have before the aprons are due," Andrea said.

Those aprons sure came in handy. "Andrea and I were talking about what kind of aprons we're going to make," I said.

"I've already started working on mine," Mary Kate said, as she sat down next to Caroline. "At least I bought the material already."

"I started mine on Monday," Caroline said. "I went right after school and bought the material and I started work on it that very night. Needlepoint takes a great deal of time, you know."

We nodded. Threading the needle takes a great deal of time for me.

"My apron's going to be really simple," Mary Kate said. "I can't do any of that fancy stuff like you can, Caroline. But Miss Collins said she'd give a good grade to someone who made a simple apron if it's well-made, so that's what I'm going to do."

"I haven't decided yet," Andrea said. "I'd like mine to be a little bit fancy, but not too much so."

"What about you, Tracy?" Caroline asked. "Have you decided what your apron's going to look like?"

I knew what it was going to look like before I even began. It was going to look like a mess. Everything I sewed looked like a mess, so why should this apron be different? But I wasn't going to say so. "I haven't made up my mind yet," I said, trying to sound like I knew what I was talking about. "I think I'll use a patterned material, though."

"Oh," Mary Kate said admiringly. "That's going to be much harder than just colored cotton."

"Oh," I said. "I haven't decided yet."

"It's a good thing we get to keep the aprons we

make," Caroline said. "Wouldn't it be awful if we had to trade them with each other, and I ended up with Tracy's?"

"Caroline!" Andrea said sharply.

"I'm not saying anything we don't already know," Caroline said. "Tracy's the worst sewer in the class. In the school, probably."

In the world, probably, I thought, but I certainly wasn't going to admit it right in front of Caroline. "I have better things to do with my time than stupid needlepoint," I said instead.

"Like what?" Caroline asked.

I'd been hoping she wouldn't. "Things," I said lamely. "Lots of things."

Caroline humphed. I almost didn't blame her.

"It's a good thing we got the tickets for the concert when we did," Mary Kate said. "I heard on the radio today they were all sold out already."

"I know," I said, happy we weren't talking about aprons anymore. "Even Scott's going, and he doesn't like Rabbit. He's taking Cheryl Ostermyer."

"Teddy Ostermyer's sister?" Caroline asked.

I nodded. "Scott's been dying to ask her out, so he ran right out and bought tickets, and she said yes."

"Is that his first date?" Caroline asked.

"Not exactly," I said. "More like his second or third. Not counting parties."

"It's going to be the most wonderful evening," Mary Kate said. "Imagine. We're actually going to see Rabbit perform live. Right here at our school."

"Yeah, it is great," Andrea said, looking hopefully at me.

It would be great all right, but not great enough. There was only one thing that would make the evening absolutely perfect, and that was really getting to meet the man I loved.

5

"Come with me when I ask Uncle Charlie?" I said to Andrea on Tuesday. That was the longest I figured I could wait.

"Oh no," she said.

"Why not?" I asked.

Andrea looked around for an answer. She finally came up with one. "Won't you do better if you go alone?" she said. "He doesn't know me. You'll seem more mature if you go alone."

The truth of the matter was I didn't want to go alone. I wasn't feeling all that mature. "Please," I said.

"No," she said.

"Sometimes I get the feeling this means a lot more to me than it does to you," I said.

"No it doesn't," she said. "I want to meet Rabbit as much as you do."

"Then why won't you go with me to see Uncle Charlie?"

"Because I think you'll be more successful if you go alone," Andrea said. "And, frankly, I don't see why you're wasting your time trying to talk me into something you know you can't, when you could be going to the newspaper and convincing Uncle Charlie to help us out."

"Oh, all right," I said. I've never been able to talk Andrea into anything if her mind is set against it. "I'll call you later to let you know how it went."

"Yeah, do," she said. "And good luck."

"Thanks a lot," I said. We parted company at the next street corner. Andrea started walking toward her apartment, and I walked downtown to the newspaper.

I couldn't remember a time when I hadn't felt right at home going to visit Dad at the paper, but this was different. First of all, I wasn't visiting Dad. I didn't even want him to know I was there. I was visiting Uncle Charlie, who I'd known all my life and loved like an uncle and right now terrified me.

I told myself I was being silly, that the worst he could do was say no. Still, I wished I had Andrea along for protection.

My father is city editor at the paper, and Uncle Charlie is managing editor. That means that Uncle Charlie is sort of Dad's boss, but neither one of them thinks of it that way. They're friends, especially ever since Uncle Charlie got his divorce. Mom tried to hide it, but she never could stand Uncle Charlie's ex-wife.

The receptionist at the paper knows me and smiled when she saw me. "Hi, Tracy," she said. "If you're here to see your father, I'm afraid you'll have to wait."

"Why, where is he?" I asked. Not with Uncle Charlie, I prayed.

"He's at a meeting with the mayor," Margie said. "They're talking about the Rabbit concert."

"Really?" I said.

"I bet you're really excited about it," Margie said. "Are you a big fan of his?"

There was no point lying about it. "I love him," I said. "I can't wait."

"I can't wait, either," Margie said. "I'm dragging my husband. He says it's just going to be a bunch of screaming kids — no insult intended, honey — but I think it'll be fun. And I love *Joyride*. I watch it every week."

"You do?" I said.

"Never miss it," she said. "I'm a little too old to squeal, but I sure intend to be there. I guess I'll see you there, then."

"I'll be there," I said. "I'm going with a whole bunch of my friends."

"That should be fun," Margie said. "I went to

a Beatles concert with friends of mine years ago. Of course we were all a little older than you are now, but it didn't matter. The place was packed. Boy, did I love Paul."

"My mother loved Marlon Brando," I said.

"Really?" Margie said. "I can't see squealing over him."

I couldn't picture my mother squealing over anybody, but I couldn't picture Margie squealing, either. It's hard picturing adults as anything other than adults. "I don't suppose you know when my dad will be getting back," I said.

"No idea, honey," Margie said. "But probably not for a while. He just left a few minutes ago."

"Oh, darn," I said, trying to sound innocent. "Well, as long as I'm here, I guess I'll say hi to Uncle Charlie. Is he busy now, do you know?"

"Charlie?" Margie said. "I don't think so. Want me to buzz him for you?"

"No, I'll just go back there and say hi," I said. "Thanks, Margie."

"It's okay, honey," she said. "I'll see you at the concert."

"I'll be looking for you," I said, and left the reception area.

I love the newspaper. To get to Uncle Charlie's office, you have to walk through an enormous room that's filled with desks and people typing and talking and cursing. There's a lot of cursing at the office, and running around, and noise. It looks like fun to work there. A lot of times I think I'll become a reporter when I grow up, or maybe an editor like Dad. I said hi to everybody I knew (which was practically everybody) and lots of people told me Dad wasn't there. I said I knew and just felt like saying hi to Uncle Charlie. I would have preferred to be more subtle about it, but it's hard to be invisible when everybody knows who you are.

Uncle Charlie was in his office sitting at his desk. He was surrounded by papers, but he always is. Managing editors keep very busy. Almost as busy as city editors, Dad says.

I knocked on his door, even though it was open, and peeked my head in. "Can I come in?" I asked him.

"Tracy," Uncle Charlie said. "Sure, come on in. Are you looking for your father?"

"No, he isn't in," I said. "He's meeting with Mayor Earle."

"Lucky man, your father," Uncle Charlie said. "Sit down. Things are frantic around here, but I always have a minute for the prettiest girl I know."

Uncle Charlie is a terrible flirt. Mom says she worries about what'll happen when I turn sixteen.

"How're things going?" I asked politely. Good manners were definitely a plus in this situation.

"Hectic," Uncle Charlie said. "Even worse than usual. You'd think this Perlman character was the first celebrity to come to this town."

"He's very famous," I said.

"So's the governor," Uncle Charlie said. "And I swear when he was here last year, there wasn't half as much fuss."

I remembered when the governor came. Dad had a headache for two days. "Everybody's really excited that Ross Perlman is coming?" I asked.

"It's been a madhouse," he said. "I don't know. What do you see in this character, anyway?"

"Oh, Uncle Charlie, he's beautiful," I said, and all of a sudden I had another wonderful idea. If Uncle Charlie went along with it, it would be the solution to all my problems. Even Dad couldn't object.

"Beautiful," Uncle Charlie grumbled. "Elizabeth Taylor was beautiful. Not some punk."

"Ross Perlman isn't a punk," I said. "He went to Dartmouth."

"So he's an educated punk," Uncle Charlie said. "That's the worst kind."

I'd had too many arguments with my father like that to get into one with Uncle Charlie. Instead, I tried the diplomatic approach. "All the kids I know really like Ross Perlman," I said.

"There's no accounting for taste," Uncle Charlie

said, and started looking at all the papers on his desk. I knew if I didn't make my move fast, I'd never have a chance.

"It's like you and Elizbabeth Taylor," I said. "Or my father and Debbie Reynolds."

"Debbie was cute," Uncle Charlie said absently. "But I preferred Liz."

"Or my mother," I said. "She just loved Marlon Brando."

Uncle Charlie looked up at me. "She did?" he said. "I guess I can see that."

"Every generation loves somebody," I said. "Mine loves Ross Perlman."

"Your entire generation loves him?" Uncle Charlie said. "Not bad."

"I guess you have lots of reporters covering the concert," I said.

"Only ten or twelve," he said. "Just a handful."

"That many?" I asked. "That's even more than you had for the governor."

"I'm kidding, Tracy," Uncle Charlie said. "Your father's assigned a couple."

"That's what I wanted to talk to you about," I said. "Maybe I should ask Dad, but I didn't want to because he's my father."

"Yeah?" Uncle Charlie said. It wasn't an encouraging yeah.

"It seems to me you should have a reporter at the concert who loves Ross Perlman," I said, trying to sound mature. "Someone who understands why all the kids love him so much."

"We do," Uncle Charlie said. "Your father assigned Linda Rosen. She's fresh out of college and she claims she never misses *Joyride*. Lord only knows why."

"She's too old," I said.

"Twenty-two is too old?" Uncle Charlie said. "It must be wonderful to be young enough to think that."

"What you need is a kid," I said. "Someone — I don't know — my age, maybe. Somebody who really loves Ross Perlman."

"Let me guess," Uncle Charlie said. "You think you'd make the perfect reporter."

"I can really write," I said. "Has Dad shown you any of my compositions?"

"Not this week," Uncle Charlie said. "Really, Tracy."

I stared at him, trying to look innocent and determined at the same time. It wasn't easy.

"Do you know how many kids have had that idea?" he said. "A dozen at least. And I admit, we gave it some thought."

"What did you decide?" I asked.

"That we'd be crazy if we did," he said. "For a lot of reasons. I'm surprised your father didn't talk to you about it."

"He didn't," I said. "Honestly. He doesn't even know I'm here. I just had this idea, and I thought I'd ask you about it."

"Every kid in town is looking for a way to meet this Perlman guy," Uncle Charlie said. "Security is going to be incredible."

"But why not send in a kid reporter?" I asked.

"If we used regular high school stringers, we might," he said. "But we don't, so we would have had to find somebody for the job. And for the one kid we picked, we would have gotten a thousand angry phone calls. No thank you."

"But nobody would mind if I did it," I said. "Dad is city editor."

"And you think nobody would mind?" he said. "They'd mind all the more for that very reason. Sorry, Tracy, but if we were going to give the job to anybody, you'd be the last one we'd pick."

"Then how about my friend Andrea?" I said. "She writes really good, too. And I know she'd be willing to do it."

"Tracy, I'm a very busy man," Uncle Charlie said. "No job for you, and none for Andrea. All right?"

"All right," I said, my face turning bright red.

"I'm going to have to tell Margie not to let any more kids in," Uncle Charlie said. "You're the third today, you know."

"I didn't know," I said. "Honestly. I just had this idea. . . ."

"You and half this town," he said. "Look, you'll see this Perlman guy at the concert. You do have tickets, don't you?"

I nodded.

"That's good," he said. "I've been getting a lot of calls about that, too. I don't know who people think I am."

"I thought you were a friend," I mumbled.

"Oh, Tracy," Uncle Charlie said. "It really isn't the end of the world if you don't get to meet him. You've lived twelve good years without meeting him. I'm sure you'll get through the next twelve just fine."

"You don't understand," I said, getting up. "I'm sorry if I took up too much of your time."

"I really do understand, Tracy," Uncle Charlie said. "And if there were anything I could do, I would, believe me. But it's just impossible. The whole situation is impossible. All right?"

"All right," I said, just wanting to get out before I started crying. "Thanks, Uncle Charlie."

"Chin up, kid," he said. "You're probably better off not meeting him."

"I don't believe that," I said.

"I don't blame you," he said. "I wouldn't have believed it if anybody told me that about Liz Taylor."

"Just one more thing?" I said.

"What, Tracy," Uncle Charlie asked, sounding impatient again.

"Could you not tell Dad I was here?" I said. "Why I came, I mean."

"Yeah," Uncle Charlie said, and smiled. "I guess I could do that for you."

I smiled back the best I could at him and walked real fast through the office, just waving good-bye to people. Margie was on the phone so I got out of the building without having to talk to her again.

Once I was on the street, I sniffled loudly, and then ran home. Running helped me feel better. It just wasn't fair. Uncle Charlie had been my best bet. He should have come through for us.

I unlocked the front door and went into the house. Nobody was home, which was fine with me. I could call Andrea in private that way, and if I cried, nobody would be around to wonder why.

I walked over to the telephone, grabbing a box

of tissues as I did. There was a note stuck on the phone.

Tracy — I had to show some people a house. Scott isn't back from track yet. You're to call Mr. Schyler at the radio station. I think you're one of the finalists.

6

Mr. Schyler told me that I was a finalist, and that I should go to the radio station Friday afternoon for the official drawing. I called Andrea immediately, and instead of telling her about my awful visit with Uncle Charlie, we concentrated on thinking lucky thoughts for me. I knew I'd win the contest; it was positively fated.

"You mean fathead," Scott said when I announced this at dinner.

But even Scott and his stupid insults couldn't bother me that night. I could hardly wait until lunch the next day to tell Caroline and Mary Kate about my incredible good luck.

"Do you really think you'll get to meet him?" Mary Kate asked.

"I hope so," I said, keeping my fingers crossed.

"What will you say to him?" she asked.

I tried to smile mysteriously. I didn't really feel like telling them that the only thing I could think to say to the man I loved was to ask if he knew Marlon Brando.

"It's no big deal talking to celebrities," Caroline said. "I've done it lots of times."

"There's a difference between talking to your father and talking to Ross Perlman," Andrea said.

"I don't mean my father," Caroline said. "But my mother gives parties for all the great artists that come here, and I always talk to them."

"But they're dull," Andrea said. "They're not wonderful like Rabbit. I bet you wouldn't be able to open your mouth if you met Rabbit."

"We'll see about that," Caroline said.

"What do you mean?" I asked. "You're not one of the finalists, are you?"

"No, of course not," Caroline said. "I wouldn't enter a dumb contest like that."

"You mean your parents wouldn't let you," Andrea said.

"I mean, thanks to my parents I don't have to do silly things like that," she said.

"Caroline, what are you talking about?" I said.

"I can't tell you," she said. "Not just yet. But you'll find out soon enough."

"I can hardly wait," Andrea said.

"I think it's wonderful that you're a finalist," Mary Kate said to me. "If you do meet him, will you get his autograph for me?"

"I'll try," I said. "But there might not be time to ask."

"Autographs are so silly," Caroline said. "Tell me Tracy, how's your apron coming?"

"My apron?" I said. I'd forgotten all about it.

"You remember the aprons," Caroline said. "It seems to me that's all you and Andrea are ever talking about."

"Oh, those aprons," I said. "Just fine."

"I've been working and working on mine," Mary Kate said. "But it still isn't as nice as Caroline's."

"Needlepoint makes such a difference," Caroline said.

"I'd like to needlepoint you one," I muttered. Andrea giggled.

"I heard that," Caroline said. "But I don't blame you for being jealous."

"I'm not jealous of anybody right now," I said. "Not even of you and your wonderful sewing. Sorry, Caroline."

Caroline sniffed. Andrea and Mary Kate giggled.

Friday was the longest day of my life. Fortunately I was supposed to go to the radio station right after school, so at least I didn't have any more time I had to kill. Getting through the school day was bad enough, and we had two tests to keep me occupied. I concentrated on them as best I could, but all I really cared about was Rabbit. I tried to think positive thoughts all day, but I knew it was just a matter of luck. Still, positive thoughts couldn't hurt.

I begged Andrea to accompany me to the radio station, and she finally agreed. She figured her mother could give her a lift home when she got off work. So we walked together, taking turns saying how I was going to win and trying to decide just what I should say to Rabbit first.

Andrea's mother only started working at the radio station last year, so the people there didn't fuss over Andrea like they do over me at the paper. That made it a lot easier for us to go to the main office and find out where the finalists were supposed to go.

"Which one of you is the finalist?" the receptionist asked.

"I am," I said.

"Then you go to Studio A," she said. "I'm afraid your friend will have to wait here."

"I'll go to Mom's office," Andrea said. "I'll meet you there."

"Okay," I said, and, after the receptionist gave me directions to Studio A, went down there. It was a little scary opening the door, but I wasn't the first one there, which made me feel better. Three other kids were standing there, along with a man.

"Hi," the man said. "I'm Rick Rogers."

Rick Rogers was the d.j. in the afternoon. "Hi," I said. "I listen to your show all the time."

"Not when you're supposed to be in school, I hope," he said and chuckled. The other kids there chuckled, too. I just smiled.

"Which one are you, honey?" he asked, looking down a sheet of paper.

"I'm Tracy Newfield," I said.

"Oh sure. Hi, Tracy," he said. "Pleased to meet you. This is Don and Lisa and Jan. We're still waiting for Evonne."

I guess she must have heard him, because at that very moment a girl opened the door.

"I guess we're through waiting," Rick Rogers said. "Okay kids, we all seem to be here. Now this is all going to be nice and easy. We're going to tape the actual lottery, and play it on the radio tonight. That way you can be sure to tell all your friends and family to listen. Tonight at 8:04, right after the news. Think you can remember that?"

We all nodded.

"Right now I'll ask you your names and where you go to school," Rick Rogers said. "Dumb things like that. And then, after we talk for a minute or so, I'll take this hat with the five entries in it and pick one. Whichever one I pick will get to meet Ross Perlman. But I'll go into those details with the winner later. There's no point boring the rest of you right now."

I wouldn't have been bored, but I knew I was going to win. It was fated.

"All right," he said. "I guess this is as good a time as any." He pressed a few buttons, then took a microphone and said in his radio voice, "Rick Rogers, Radio's Royalty here, and I have with me five really nice kids, nice lookers, too, all of them. And these five are WRAL's five lucky finalists in our 'Meet the Rabbit Contest.' One of them will get to meet Ross Perlman himself, and the other four will just have to be satisfied meeting me. No, seriously, they'll all get copies of Ross's hit album *Perlman's Pearls*, which we'll be featuring as our album of the week tomorrow night at eleven o'clock. Meantime, why don't I say hello to these kids, let them introduce themselves to you."

He thrust the microphone in one of the girl's faces. I thanked heaven I wasn't the first one to go.

"And what's your name, dear?" Rick Rogers asked her.

"Jan Shulman," she said.

"Well, Jan, it's a real pleasure to meet you," he said. "Tell me, how old are you?"

"I'm sixteen," she said.

"Sixteen," he said. "Does your boyfriend know you entered the contest?"

"Yes, of course," she said.

"And he isn't jealous?" Rick Rogers asked.

Jan just stared at him.

"Now over here we have another lovely girl," he said. "And your name is . . .?"

"Lisa Milligan," she said.

"And how old are you, Lisa?" he asked.

"Fourteen," she said.

"Fourteen. Nice age," Rick Rogers said. "I see you have a Rabbit button on."

Lisa nodded.

"It's a nice button, folks," Rick Rogers said. "It's about two inches wide and it has a big color picture of Ross Perlman. You plan on wearing that if you get to meet him?"

"I don't know," Lisa said.

"I'm sure he'd get a big kick out of it if you did," Rick Rogers said. "Over here we have our only male contestant. You're Don Smith, right?"

"Right," Don said.

"And what grade are you in, Don?" Rick Rogers asked.

"I'm a sophomore," he said.

"Tell me, why does a boy want to meet Ross Perlman so much?" Rick Rogers asked.

"I think Rabbit is cool," Don said. "Besides, my girl friend said she'd make out with me if I introduced her to him."

"Good reason," Rick Rogers said. "This young lady is our youngest contestant. Tell me, what is your name, honey?"

I knew he meant me because he slammed the microphone under my nose. "I'm Tracy Newfield," I said.

"And how old are you, Tracy?"

"Twelve."

"Twelve," he said. "Do your parents know you're here?"

"I told them I was coming," I said. "Besides, by the time they hear this I'll be home with them."

"Yes, of course," he said. "Now our fifth and final contestant is this lovely young lady. And you're . . .?"

"Evonne Marlowe," she said.

"And you're how old, dear?"

"I'm fourteen," she said.

"Another fourteen-year-old," he said. "Do you love Rabbit?"

"Oh, yes," she said.

"Well, in just a moment you'll find out if you're going to be the lucky one who's going to get to meet Ross Perlman," Rick Rogers said. "What we've done here is put all five finalists' entries in this handsome hat. By the way, I want to say that I was lucky enough to read many of the entries that you wonderful fans sent in to us, and believe me, I didn't envy the judges having to come up with just five finalists. There are a lot of interesting people out there with a lot of interesting reasons for wanting to meet Ross Perlman. I know the judges really sweated it out, trying to decide who should be our five finalists. But eventually they did decide, and as you've heard, all five finalists are eager to meet the Rabbit. And to tell you the truth, I don't blame them. Ross Perlman is one talented son of a gun. Don here, as my only male companion, I want you to come over and verify that there are five slips of paper in this hat."

"Yeah, there are," Don said.

"We copied each of the prize-winning entries onto paper to make them easier to fold," Rick Rogers said. "Now I'll just close my eyes and pick a name out of the hat."

Oh, let me win, I prayed. Please let me win.

"This is fun, folks," Rick Rogers said, grabbing a piece of paper out of the hat. "All right, it's time for me to open my eyes and let the world know which of these five talented teens is going to meet Ross Perlman."

Please let it be me.

"And here's our winning entry," Rick Rogers announced. " 'I want to meet Ross Perlman, the Rabbit, because ever since he hopped into my life, I've been harebrained about him.' " Congratulations, Jan Shulman, for your clever, award-winning entry. I guess your boyfriend will be really jealous now!"

"I didn't win?" Lisa said. I was real glad she got the words out before I did.

"I'm afraid not," Rick Rogers said. "Of course each of you four runners-up will get copies of Ross Perlman's album *Perlman's Pearls*. That's our featured album of the week this Saturday night at eleven. I guess you'll be able to play your albums along with the radio."

Lisa looked as stricken as I felt.

"Now I want to thank each and every one of you wonderful kids," Rick Rogers said, "and all you kids out there who entered our contest and didn't get to be finalists. And I'm sure I'll see all of you at the Ross Perlman concert."

We just stared at him.

Rick Rogers pressed some more buttons and put the mike away. "Now kids, if you all just go to the main office, the receptionist will have your albums waiting for you," he said. "Except for you, Jan. I'll fill you in on the details, and then we'll tape a few spontaneous comments from you. Okay, the rest of you can go."

We continued to stare at him.

"Thanks again," he said. "You were all great. And don't forget to listen to yourselves tonight at 8:04. And be sure to tell your friends."

"And families," Don said.

"And families," Rick Rogers said.

Don led us out of the studio. We all walked to the main office in silence.

"I thought I'd win," Lisa said.

"I knew I'd win," I said.

"It was probably fixed," Don said. "Oh well. Who wants to meet that creep, anyway?"

There was no point telling him. Besides, I didn't feel like talking ever again for the rest of my whole life. If I couldn't meet Ross Perlman, I had nothing to tell the world.

7

"I thought you sounded very nice," Mom said that evening, after we'd listened to Rick Rogers and me on the radio. I hadn't wanted to, but Mom and Dad insisted. Even Scott said he'd like to hear me on the radio.

"You didn't say very much," Dad said.

"I only wish you'd be that way here," Scott said.

"Don't tease," Mom said. "Honey, I know you're disappointed. But it's not the end of the world."

If it wasn't, I wanted to know what was. But there was no point saying so.

The phone rang. "One of Tracy's fans," Scott said, getting up to answer it. "Oh, hi," he said. "It's Andrea," he told me with a grimace.

I walked slowly to the phone. Andrea had offered me a few words of comfort at the radio station. I couldn't think why she was calling.

"I thought you sounded very good on the radio," she said, after we'd said hello.

"Do you have the album?" she asked.

"Yeah, they gave it to me before I left the radio station," I said. "Why?"

"I was wondering if you could give me the picture album that's in it for my scrapbook," she said.

I had to think for a second; then it came back to me. Inside the record jacket was an eight-page album of pictures of Ross. Andrea had a copy of the album, too, but had decided not to cut the pictures out of the album, to keep it whole.

"Sure," I said. "I don't need another album."

"Thanks," she said. "I'll bring the scrapbook over to your house tomorrow morning, and we can put the pictures in together.

"Fine," I said. "I'll see you then."

"You sound so sad," she said.

"I am," I said.

"Look, I'm not going to meet him, either," she said. "At least we won't be meeting him together."

I managed a little smile. "Thanks, Andrea," I said. "I'll see you tomorrow."

I slumped my way back into the living room when the phone rang again. I stared helplessly at Scott, who went into the kitchen to answer it. "Tracy Newfield Fan Club," he said. There was a pause. "Oh, sure, Caroline. I'll get the star."

I moved back to the kitchen. "Is this going to be going on all night?" Scott asked. "The rest of us might want to get a phone call, too, you know."

I waved him out of the room while greeting Caroline.

"I heard you on the radio," she said. "My parents thought you behaved very maturely."

Just what I needed to hear. "They listened, too?" I said.

"I made them," she said. "Tracy, what do you want more than anything else in the whole world?"

"To meet Rabbit," I said. "You know that."

"What if I told you that could be arranged?"

"Caroline, what are you talking about?" I demanded.

"Remember I was hinting about something at lunch the other day?" she said. "About meeting stars?"

"I remember," I said.

"I couldn't say anything then, because it wasn't definite, but my parents talked to Mr. Thomas and he said they could give the party. He's a widower, you know."

"Caroline, what are you saying?"

"Mr. Thomas is a widower and he doesn't like giving big parties. Naturally, my parents are the most logical people to give a party for Ross Perlman if Mr. Thomas won't, so *they're* giving the party. After the concert next Friday. What do you think about that?"

I thought I would die on the spot. "And you're going to get to meet him?" I said, trying hard not to cry. "Ross Perlman is going to be at your house and you're going to meet him?"

I could hear Caroline smirking. "You got it," she said. "I'll serve him canapés and everything."

Ross loved canapés. I remembered reading that somewhere. "Oh, Caroline," I said. I knew I should be happy for her, but I didn't have it in me.

"Hold on," she said. "I told my parents I wanted to have you come to the party, too, because you're my very best friend in the world."

"Yeah?" I said, my heart starting to thump wildly. "What did they say?"

"First they said absolutely not," Caroline said. "Mom was afraid you'd make a scene. Pour Scotch over Ross or something. So I had them listen to you on the radio, and Mom and Dad agreed you behaved very maturely."

"And. . . ." I could hardly breathe.

"And they said if you absolutely swore not to faint or do anything really stupid, you could come to the party and meet Ross," Caroline said triumphantly.

"Oh my gosh," I said.

"What are you going to wear?" she asked. "Mom's letting me buy a whole new outfit. Purple, I think, so don't wear anything that will clash."

The last thing I could concentrate on was clashing color schemes. "Ross is going to be at your house, and I'm invited?" I said, just to make sure.

"Only if you want to," Caroline said. "Of course, if you have other plans for that night. . . ."

Plans. It all came back to me. "Caroline," I said. "Wait a second. Does it have to be me alone?"

"You won't be alone," she said. "I'll be there."

"No, I mean Andrea," I said. "Can't she come, too?"

"I didn't invite Andrea. I invited you."

"Yes, I know, and I appreciate it so much, but can't Andrea come, too?" I hated begging Caroline for anything, but this time I had to.

"I don't think you understand," Caroline said. "I had to fight with my parents for practically a whole evening before they'd even listen to you on that dumb radio show. They didn't want me to invite anybody. They hardly even want me to come. Now you expect me to ask them to let Andrea come, too?"

"Caroline, please," I said. "It's so important to me."

"Why?" she said coldly.

"We made a pact," I said. "Andrea and I. We swore we'd meet Rabbit together."

"I don't believe it," Caroline said. "I'm offering you a chance to meet Ross Perlman, to talk with him at a party at my parents' house, and you're saying no because of some dumb pact?"

"I didn't say I'd say no," I said. "I just asked if Andrea could come, too."

"She can't," Caroline said. "If I asked my parents, they'd say I couldn't come, either, and I'd have to spend the night at my aunt's house."

"Oh, Caroline," I said.

"Are you going to come to the party, or aren't you?" she asked. "Make up your mind, Tracy."

"Let me think for a minute, okay?" I said. I wished we had a hold button; I would have enjoyed putting Caroline on hold for about twenty years. Ten years for me to make up my mind, and another ten years for me to forgive myself for whatever I decided. Because I knew I'd hate myself no matter what I told Caroline.

I thought for a moment about going in to the living room and letting Mom and Dad tell me what to do, but I knew I couldn't. First of all, I knew Dad would tell me to say no, and I was pretty sure Mom would tell me that, too, Marlon Brando or no Marlon Brando. Besides, if I went around complaining all the time that they treated me like a kid, I could hardly go to them and behave like one.

"Well?" Caroline said.

"I'm thinking," I said.

"I haven't got all day," she said. "Honestly, Tracy, sometimes I wonder why you are my best friend."

That did it. If I said yes, I'd be stuck with Caroline as a best friend for the rest of my life. Not even Ross Perlman was worth that.

"Caroline, I just can't," I said. "A pact is a pact."

"You idiot!" she shrieked. "What do you expect me to tell my parents?"

"Tell them the truth," I said. "Then maybe they'll let Andrea come, too."

"I'll tell them no such thing," she said. "Goodbye, Tracy, and go to blazes!" She hung up the phone.

I stared at it for a moment, and then I hung up the receiver. If this wasn't the worst day of my life, I couldn't imagine a worse one. I waited to see if feeling self-righteous would make me feel better, but I couldn't even work up a sensation of nobility. I felt just rotten.

"What was that all about?" Dad asked, when I went back to the living room. "You look like the walking plague."

I told them, leaving out all the parts about how Andrea and I had planned on getting to meet Rabbit. I may have felt miserable, but I wasn't crazy.

"Poor baby," Mom said. "But you did the right thing."

"I know," I said. Maybe pity would make me feel better. "But I wanted to meet him so much."

"Maybe you will, anyway," Scott said.

We all turned toward him.

"I don't know," he said defensively. "But it seems to me Tracy got awfully close twice. Maybe the third time she'll get lucky."

That was the nicest thing Scott had ever said to me in twelve years. I just wished I could believe it.

"Stranger things have happened," Dad said.

"Yeah, sure," I said. "Maybe he'll get a flat tire right outside our house."

"Just as long as he doesn't expect me to help him change it," Dad said. Dad hates changing tires.

"Maybe you'll come up with a way to meet him that has nothing to do with Caroline," Mom said. "Or maybe Andrea will come up with an idea."

I thought about mentioning covering it for the paper, but decided against it. Everybody was feeling nice and sorry for me, but I knew better than to press my luck.

"You made a very difficult decision," Dad said. He put his right hand under my chin, and lifted my head up. "And while you might not believe it now, in the long run you'll be a lot happier with the choice you made than you would if you'd accepted Caroline's invitation."

"I know," I said. "I'm just so miserable."

The phone rang. "Maybe that's Rabbit, now," Scott said, getting up for a third time. "Maybe he heard you on the radio and decided you were the one he wanted to meet."

I was such an idiot, I started feeling hopeful again. "Oh, hi," Scott said. "I'll tell her you're calling." He came back into the living room, and said, "This time it's Mary Kate."

My heart sank. I felt like a total fool. I walked back to the kitchen and made a solemn vow never to get another phone call again.

"Hi," I said slowly. "What do you want?"

"Tracy, what's the matter?" Mary Kate asked. "You sound awful."

"I feel awful," I said, but I realized I didn't want to go into it. For all I knew, Mary Kate thought she was Caroline's best friend, and I was in no mood to cause any trouble. "I guess it's just from losing the contest."

"I heard you on the radio," she said. "I thought you sounded best. You should have won."

"They didn't decide it that way," I said.

"I guess not," she said. "If they had, you would have won. I was really proud that I knew you."

"Thanks, Mary Kate," I said. Everybody was proud of me that night. Fat lot of good it was doing me.

"So how's your apron coming along?" she asked.

"Apron?" I said.

"For home ec?" she said. "You keep forgetting."

"I remember," I said. It was amazing how easy it was to forget about that apron.

"It's due in next Friday," Mary Kate said. "How's it coming?"

"I haven't done anything," I said. "I haven't even bought the material."

"Oh, Tracy," Mary Kate said. "And the way you sew, too."

"There're more important things than sewing," I said angrily. "Life's a lot more important than some dumb old apron!" And I slammed the phone down fast before Mary Kate had a chance.

8

"It's not the end of the world," Andrea said to me the next morning.

"What isn't?" I said.

"Not winning the contest," she said.

"Oh, that," I said. The contest seemed like a long time ago to me already. "I know," I said.

"You've been so quiet all morning," she said.

"I've had things on my mind," I said. "Like helping you choose which pictures to put in your scrapbook."

"I think we did a good job," she said, staring with satisfaction at our work. "Rabbit would be proud."

"He'll never know," I said bitterly. I hadn't told Andrea about Caroline's invitation because I didn't want her to feel bad that I couldn't meet him because of her. If I was going to be noble, I might as well be noble all the way.

"Maybe something will happen," she said. "He

is going to be right here at Taft. We can always wait around afterward and maybe he'll give us his autograph."

"I wanted more than an autograph," I said. "I wanted to talk to him, to tell him how much I love him."

"Maybe we should write him letters," Andrea said. "After the concert. We could tell him how much we love him and how good he was, and maybe he'll invite us to Hollywood to meet him."

I stared at her. "You don't honestly believe that'll happen, do you?" I asked.

"No," she said. "But I was hoping you might, and then you wouldn't be so grumpy. Which picture do you think I should choose?"

I looked at the two pictures. One was of Ross as a little boy, the other of him in his first movie role. "The one when he was a kid," I said. "His first movie was really awful."

"Okay," Andrea said, and started cutting. She was a very good cutter. Watching her with a scissors made me think of my apron. But not for very long.

The phone rang. "I'll get it!" I shouted, and ran to my parents' bedroom to answer it. It was Andrea's mother, so I called for Andrea to come. I left her alone and went back to my bedroom to check the scrapbook out. It really was wonderful. All it was was a plain old looseleaf notebook, but Andrea had pasted pictures of Ross all over the cover, and she must have had over a hundred pages of pictures and articles about Ross in it. It would be nice to have his autograph.

"I have to go home," Andrea said, running into my room.

"Why?" I asked, and got up. She looked like she was in an awful hurry.

"I have to baby-sit with Mikey," she said. "I forgot, but my parents are having lunch with my aunt and uncle today. No kids invited. I think they're going to say they're getting a divorce."

"Your parents are getting a divorce?" I asked, and followed Andrea downstairs.

"No, silly, my aunt and uncle," Andrea said, getting her jacket. "They fight all the time. And my aunt's left my uncle twice since Christmas. Besides, why else wouldn't they want Mikey and me to come?"

"Beats me," I said.

"Don't be so unhappy," she said, opening the front door. "I'll talk to you later."

"Sure," I said, and closed the door behind her. It was an ugly, gray day, and it matched my mood.

"If you're going to sulk all day, why don't you

do it in your room?" Mom said to me. "Not that I'd mind your company, if you'd just cheer up a little."

"I'll never cheer up," I said.

"Then go to your room," she said. "You could make Pollyanna depressed."

So I went back upstairs, and found Andrea's scrapbook right in the middle of my floor.

For a moment I thought about going to her house and working on it with her there, but that would have meant spending an afternoon with Mikey, and I was in no mood for that. He's seven years old and just awful. So I took my scissors, and put the notebook on my desk. Then I climbed on my bed and stared at the ceiling for a while. If life was this bad when I was twelve, what would it be like when I was twenty?

After a while I got bored lying on my bed and being miserable. Besides, if I wasn't doing anything, I didn't have any excuse not to be working on my apron. And the first thing I'd have to do for that was buy the material (not that I knew how much I'd need), and that would mean leaving the house, and I didn't want to do that just in case Caroline called and said her parents had said it was okay for me to bring Andrea to their party. So I had to get up and do something. It took me a while to decide just what, but I finally decided on reading a book in the living room with Mom. So I picked one off my shelves and went back down.

"Feeling better?" Mom asked.

"I'm not feeling worse," I said. "Will that do?"

"I suppose it'll have to," she said. She was reading a magazine.

We sat there quietly for a while, both of us reading. Dad and Scott were out shopping. It was really kind of nice, and pretty soon I was feeling better about life. Sure, I wasn't going to get to meet the Rabbit, but then again, I'd never met him so I didn't know what I was missing. Besides, maybe he was horrible and I was better off not knowing. I read an article about him once that said he was a real snob, but I didn't believe it. Maybe I should have.

I finished the book I was reading, and decided to go upstairs. Dad and Scott came in as I was on my way up, so I waved hello, but kept on walking. I thought maybe I'd clean my closet; I was in the mood to throw things out. Besides, I thought I might have a picture of Caroline someplace, and I wanted to destroy it.

It took me a while to find the picture, and I was looking at it, trying to decide just what miserable things to do to it, when the phone rang. I could hear Mom and Dad and Scott talking, so I went into my parents' room to answer it.

"Hello?"

"Hi, Tracy? This is Andrea."

"Oh, hi," I said, settling down on the bed. Mikey must be entertaining himself, and that meant Andrea and I would have plenty of time to talk. "What's new?"

"Tracy, you'll never believe it," Andrea said, and I could hear how excited she was. "I'm going to get to meet Rabbit!"

"What?" I said. "How? What are you talking about?"

"It's just incredible," she said. "Caroline called me and her parents are giving a party for Ross and she said they said she could bring just one friend to the party and she asked me. Isn't that incredible?"

It was a good thing I was sitting down. I felt the room spinning all around me as it was.

"Tracy, are you still there?" Andrea said.

"Party?" I said. That was all I could say.

"She said that first she'd asked somebody else but she wasn't interested — can you imagine that? I wonder who it was. Not Mary Kate. She'd give her right arm to meet Ross. Anyway, whoever it was said no, so Caroline asked her parents if it would be okay if she asked somebody else instead, and they said okay just as long as she was mature, and Caroline said I was the most mature person she knew. I always thought you were very mature, but you know Caroline. So I'm going to get to go and to meet Ross! Is there anything you want me to tell him for you?"

I could think of a lot of things, but I wasn't sure Andrea knew just what those words meant. "Andrea, are you serious?" I finally choked out.

"You think Caroline is teasing me?" Andrea said. "I don't. She's crazy, but I don't think she'd do anything that mean. Why should she?"

"What about our pact?"

"What pact?" Andrea asked, just a little too brightly. I knew she was lying.

"You know what pact!" I screamed. "The one we made together. We'd either meet him together or not at all."

"Oh, that pact," Andrea said. "I didn't think you'd mind.

"Mind?"

"It was your idea," she said.

"It was not!"

"Oh," Andrea said. "I thought it was. Anyway, I knew you wouldn't mind. If you had a chance to meet him and I didn't, I certainly wouldn't mind."

"I did have a chance," I said. "Caroline asked me first, and I said no. Because of our pact. Because of our friendship."

"Well, you shouldn't have," she said. "I wouldn't have minded; I just told you that."

"I took our pact seriously," I said.

"Oh, come on," she said. "If you'd won the radio contest, and they said you couldn't bring me along, would you have refused to go?"

"I don't know," I said.

"See," she said.

"Now wait a second," I said. "I didn't say I would have, just that I don't know. There's a difference."

"You would have gone," Andrea said. "And I wouldn't have minded. How many chances are you going to have to meet Rabbit?"

"I might not have gone," I said. "Besides, that has nothing to do with this. Caroline invited me first, and I said no. I think you should call her back and say you can't go."

"Are you crazy?" Andrea said. "I'm not going to do that."

"I don't believe this," I said.

"You of all people should understand," she said. "You were the one who was so crazy for us to go. You were the one who came up with all the crazy ideas."

"They weren't crazy," I said. "And I did most of them myself. All you had to do was call Mr. Thomas."

There was a silence at the other end.

"You did call Mr. Thomas, didn't you?" I asked.

"Oh, Tracy," Andrea said.

"You didn't?"

"I couldn't," she said. "Besides, he wouldn't have helped us even if I had called."

"But you said you called," I said.

"What was I supposed to say?" she asked. "You wouldn't listen to me when I told you I couldn't. He's my father's client! My father would have absolutely killed me."

"So you lied to me, too," I said.

"Calm down," Andrea said. "If I thought Mr. Thomas would have helped, I would have called him. But I knew he wouldn't, and I just couldn't risk having my father find out. It just wasn't worth it."

"So I did everything and you did nothing and you're going to get to meet Rabbit," I said. "Talk about fair."

"So maybe it isn't fair," Andrea said. "But you had your chance. Caroline asked you first."

"But I said no because of our pact," I said.

"You could have asked me first," Andrea said. "I would have told you to say yes. You just weren't smart enough to think of that."

"I hate you," I said. "You're a rotten, miserable little creep. I hope you die."

"That's an awful thing to say, Tracy," Andrea said.

"I said it and I meant it," I said.

"Well, I hope you die, too," she said.

I slammed the phone down fast because I didn't want her to have the satisfaction of hanging up on me. I stared at the phone for a moment. I never hated anybody so much before in my life. I found I was shaking.

"Tracy, what was that all about?" Mom called from downstairs. I guess I'd been pretty loud.

"Leave me alone!" I screamed, and ran out of her room and into mine. I slammed my door real hard, and waited to start crying.

But I didn't cry. I was still too angry. And seeing Andrea's Rabbit scrapbook made me even angrier.

I walked over slowly to my desk and picked the notebook up. I opened it and pressed the lever down so all the pages could come out. Carefully at first, and then faster and more wildly, I started tearing up each and every picture of Ross Perlman. I hated him and I hated the radio station and that miserable Rick Rogers and I hated Caroline and mostly I hated Andrea. I tore up each page into fours, and then I tore them up again, so there wasn't a single picture of Ross that stayed together. Soon I found myself surrounded with Ross Perlman confetti, thousands of little pieces of pictures of him all over my floor, all over me. And then I cried.

9

"I'm sure all you girls have finished work on your aprons by now," Miss Collins said in home ec Thursday afternoon. "And I'm looking forward to seeing all of them here tomorrow."

Aprons! All of a sudden I realized I was expected to hand in a fully sewn apron the very next day, and I hadn't even bought the material yet. I had just gotten through the awfulest week I could imagine, and my mind hadn't been able to focus on anything, let alone aprons.

"Mine's all done," Caroline said smugly.

For about the fiftieth time that week, I kept myself from slugging her. It would have been closer to a hundred times except I saw as little of her as I possibly could. Instead of having lunch with her and Mary Kate and Andrea the way I had for years, I ate alone, or with other kids. I checked them out a lot, though. Only Caroline seemed to be happy that week. Mary Kate was sulking about something, probably not being asked to the party, and Andrea looked miserable. It served her right. Besides, she couldn't possibly be as miserable as I was. It was all her fault, anyway. I just hoped she suffered for the rest of her natural born days as much as she'd made me suffer.

I'd thought all weekend about taking my Rabbit confetti to school on Monday and throwing it at Andrea, but I figured that would just get me in trouble. So Monday morning I took a sandwich bag's worth, including parts of Andrea's favorite pictures, and before school I walked up to her and handed it over.

"This is yours," I said, real cool. "The rest of it is at my house, if you want it back."

It took Andrea a few moments to figure out what it was I'd just given her. Then her eyes got real big.

"You didn't," she said.

"I sure did," I said. "It took me over an hour to do it, too. I tore up every single picture in your stupid scrapbook."

"But it took me years — " she sputtered. "How could you?"

"Real easy," I said. "Let me know if you want the rest, or if I should just burn it." And then I walked away.

I thought that would make me feel better about

things, but it didn't. I was still miserable.

Hating Andrea and feeling sorry for myself took up a lot of my time that week. The only thing that cheered me up was thinking about sitting next to Andrea during the concert and showering her with confetti for the whole evening. I checked it out, and I figured if I was real careful with how much I threw at her, I could make it last from the first song to the last.

But here it was Thursday already, and I didn't have anything remotely resembling an apron. And I couldn't cheat and buy a nice simple one, because the way I sewed, if I handed in anything that didn't look terrible, I'd get caught. So after school I went to the five-and-ten and bought a couple of yards of yellow cotton. I was terrified that Andrea would see me buying the material and make fun of me for not having gotten the apron done yet, so I didn't look at the fan magazines or comic books. I just bought the material and ran home.

Once I got in, I realized I didn't have the slightest idea how to sew an apron. Miss Collins had taught us how to do it way back, but I hadn't listened. Why should I? I was never going to have to sew an apron again. Ordinarily, I would have called Andrea and asked her how to do it, and then maybe she would have come over and we would have spent the evening with her coaching me on the fine points of sewing, and giggling about the concert. But I couldn't do that. And I couldn't ask Mom, who didn't know how to sew an apron either, and would have gotten mad at me if she found out I'd had almost three weeks to do the assignment and I'd left it to the very last minute.

"Hey, Scott," I said. Any port in a storm.

"Yeah, what?" he said.

Actually, Scott had been pretty nice to me all week. He'd hardly teased me at all. I guess that was because every time he tried, I started crying, and that upset Mom and Dad. It upset me a lot more.

"Do you know how to sew an apron?" I asked him.

"Are you crazy?" he asked. Then he shook his head sadly. "Stupid question. Of course you are."

The tears started welling.

"Hold on," he said. "What's the problem?"

"I have to sew this apron by tomorrow, and I don't even know how to do it," I said. "And I can't ask Andrea."

"No, I guess you can't," he said. "Well, do you have any material?"

"Of course," I said, and got the bag. I opened it, and unfurled the cotton.

"Sure is yellow," Scott said. "I guess that's enough material."

"What should I do?" I asked.

Scott looked thoughtful. "It seems to me when you sew you need patterns," he said.

"I don't have a pattern for an apron," I said. "Do you think Mom does?"

"Are you — " he began. "Oh, forget it. No, I don't think Mom has a pattern. But I bet she has an apron. Maybe you should look at it, and then we could figure out how to make one."

"Scott, you're a genius," I said, and ran into the kitchen. It took a little searching, but I found an apron, and brought it back to the living room for Scott's inspection.

"This doesn't look too complicated," Scott said, examining the apron. "Just a piece of material and a sash. And a pocket. You don't need a pocket, do you?"

"I'll check my notes," I said, but when I did, all I found were doodles of rabbits. "I don't think I have to make a pocket," I told Scott. "I remember Miss Collins said plain was okay."

"Fine," Scott said. "Why don't we use the apron as a pattern."

"What do you mean?" I asked.

"Let's trace Mom's apron onto this piece of material," he said. "Like it was a pattern. And then you just cut from the tracing, and you'll have an apron. Complete with sash. What do you think?"

"I think you're the best big brother in the entire world," I said. I would have hugged him, except I knew he would have slugged me. So I got a magic marker instead, and traced the apron as best I could onto the material. Then I got a scissors and cut where I had traced. Scott watched carefully as I worked.

"What do you think?" I asked when I finished. I picked up my newly made apron and showed it to him.

"I don't know," he said. "It looks like an apron to me. You sure Miss Collins won't mind if it's plain?"

"Not if it's well-made," I said.

"It's all one piece," he said. "Do you think you could do better?"

I shook my head.

"Then you might as well hand it in," he said. "At least you'll have something."

"Do you think she'll mind the magic marker showing?" I asked. I'd tried to cut it all off, but I just wasn't as good with scissors as Andrea.

"I don't see why she should," Scott said. "I think it's kind of nice. It makes it look a little less yellow."

"That's because I used purple magic marker," I said. "I figured it would show up better."

"I think it's fine," he said. "Just as long as you never expect me to wear it."

"Nobody's ever going to have to wear it," I said, starting to clean the living room so Mom wouldn't be upset when she got home. "I'll throw it out as soon as I get it back from Miss Collins."

"Then it should do just fine," he said. "Any more problems?"

"None," I said. "And thank you."

"Any time," he said, looking very pleased with himself. And I don't mind that he did.

School on Friday took forever. It would have been interminable, anyway, with all of us waiting for the concert that night, but it seemed to take even longer because of how rotten I felt every time I saw Andrea and Caroline and thought about them going to the party and getting to meet Rabbit in person. Still, I felt relief that I had an apron to hand in. Sure, it might not be as pretty as Caroline's, but at least it was finished, and that was more than I thought possible the day before.

Miss Collins decided to have us hand in our aprons the very last thing. She went from girl to girl, clucking her approval over each one as she took it. Caroline's she showed to all of us. It had flowers embroidered all over it and I guess it looked pretty good.

She got to me last, right before the period ended.

"Now Tracy," she said. "Let's see what you've come up with."

I knew my apron wasn't as good as anybody else's, but I still wasn't expecting her reaction. Miss Collins took one look at my apron and said, "Good Lord."

Everybody laughed, Caroline hardest of all. I felt ready to cry all over again.

"Did you — no you didn't, you didn't sew a single stitch," she said, turning the apron around. "You just cut it out of whole cloth. I don't believe this."

"You said you wouldn't mind if it was simple," I whispered.

"I said simple, not simpleminded," Miss Collins said. "Really, Tracy. I knew you'd hand me a third-rate piece of work, but I never expected anything as awful as this. And there isn't even a pocket."

The bell rang. Everybody gathered their books together.

"All right, class, you're all dismissed," Miss Collins said. "Except for you, Tracy."

Everyone left. I thought I saw Andrea look sympathetically at me, but it was hard to tell, since my eyes were full of tears.

"Honestly, Tracy," Miss Collins said once we were alone. "Did you really think I'd let you get away with something like this?"

"I can't sew," I said, trying hard not to cry in front of her. "Nobody in my family can."

"I don't know about your family and, frankly, I don't much care," Miss Collins said. "You may just think this is home ec, and it doesn't count, but it does. It's a class, the same as any other. You wouldn't hand in an English paper like this, would you?"

I shook my head.

"I have no choice but to tell you to stay after school today and finish this thing," she said. "Cut that — that sash off, and hem the apron so that you can't see any of that purple stuff, and then hem the sash and sew it back onto the apron. I'll forget about the pocket. If you do all that, I'll give you a D. Otherwise it's an F, and with an F on your apron, you'll fail home ec this semester. Do you want that?"

"No," I mumbled.

"All right," she said. "Here's yellow thread and a needle and pins and scissors. I'm going to leave you here because I have other things to do right now, but I'll be back this evening for the concert. I expect to find the apron on my desk when I get here, a half hour before the concert begins. Deal?"

"Deal," I said.

"Good," she said. "Good luck, Tracy. And remember, you can do anything if you really want to."

Except sew, I thought, but I didn't say so. Instead, I tried to smile at her. Miss Collins put all the other aprons into a big shopping bag and left me alone.

I stared at the apron and the thread for a while and felt just like Cinderella. I wouldn't have time to go home before the concert and get the confetti to throw at Andrea. I was surprised at how little that bothered me. I hated hating Andrea.

I was busy trying to thread the needle when I heard somebody at the door. The school was still full of people preparing for the concert, so I wasn't worried, but I did look up to see who it was. It was Andrea.

"What do you want?" I asked.

"To apologize," she said. "Can I come in?"

I nodded.

"You're right," she said shrugging her shoulders. "I've been thinking about it all week, and I shouldn't have accepted Caroline's invitation. At least not before I talked to you about it."

"I shouldn't have torn up your scrapbook," I said.

"You were mad at me," she said. "And I don't blame you. Anyway, I just told Caroline I wouldn't be going to her stupid party after all."

"Really?" I said.

"I couldn't stand the way she was behaving all week," Andrea said. "She kept putting her arm around me and saying we were best friends. I hate Caroline. Besides, you're my best friend."

"You're mine, too," I said.

"Caroline's going to ask Mary Kate instead," Andrea said. "But she's going to tell her parents she's me. She says they can't tell her friends apart, anyway."

I giggled. Boy, it felt good giggling with Andrea again.

"I don't suppose I could help you with the apron," Andrea said.

"No, you'd better not," I said.

"Want my company?"

"No," I said. "Because if I'm talking to you, I'll never get it done."

"It is pretty funny-looking," Andrea said. "Okay, I'll leave you alone. But we'll sit next to each other at the concert, okay?"

"Great," I said. "Andrea, I'm so glad we're friends again."

"Me, too," she said. "I'll see you later."

I nodded, and watched as she left the room. Working on the apron didn't seem nearly so bad after that. I cut the sash off, got the thread through the needle, and was bent over, hard at work, hemming the apron so the magic marker didn't show, when once again I heard someone at the door. I was sure it was Miss Collins, checking up on me, so I almost didn't look. But as soon as I did, I promptly stuck the needle into my thumb.

Standing at the doorway, all by himself, was Ross Perlman.

10

"Excuse me," Rabbit said, "but is this the home ec room?"

Only he didn't sound like Rabbit. He sounded the way he did on talk shows: soft-spoken and smart.

"I was told to come to the home ec room to rest up before the concert," he said. "Is this it?"

There was no point trying to say anything, so I just nodded.

"Good," he said, coming in. "Although I wasn't expecting anybody to be here."

"I'm sewing an apron," I said. "If I don't finish sewing it today, I'm going to flunk home ec."

"Oh, then keep on sewing," he said, putting his overnight bag down. "I don't want to make you flunk anything." He said that like Rabbit, though, and I could tell he was teasing.

"I'm really very smart," I said. "I just can't sew. Nobody in my family can."

"It's a useful thing to be able to do," he said. "My mother taught me before I went to college. Her motto is 'Be prepared,' just like the Boy Scouts."

"My mother would have taught me, but she hates sewing," I said. I could not believe I was carrying on this conversation. "But my father went to Dartmouth."

"Hey, really?" he said. "So did I."

"I know," I said. "Everybody knows that."

"Oh," he said. "But does everybody know I nearly flunked physics my freshman year, and only passed because I did an extra assignment? Like you're doing?"

"No," I said. "Nobody knows that. Except me."

"Tell you what," he said. "You don't tell anybody that, and I won't tell anybody about your apron."

I laughed, then looked down at my apron. My thumb was bleeding.

"Oh," I said, holding up the thumb. "Look at that."

"Oh," Ross said. "Hey, I carry Band Aids with me. 'Be prepared' and all that." He opened his bag and searched through it, until he found a little package of them. Then he got up and brought them over to me.

"Thank you," I said, and took the package. I

managed to get one Band Aid out, without shaking too hard, and handed the box back to him. Somehow I tore the paper covering off, and got the Band Aid on. Ross took the paper and tossed it in Miss Collins' wastepaper basket and then sat down again. Our hands had touched. I was surprised I didn't die on the spot.

"That's a pretty apron,' he said. "Yellow is my favorite color."

"Really?" I said, trying to sew again. If I didn't sew, I wouldn't have any excuse to stay there, and I sure wasn't about to leave.

"You mean everybody doesn't know that?" he asked.

I sighed. "Yeah, they do," I said. "I was just being polite."

Ross laughed. I made him laugh! Rather than get hysterical, I kept sewing.

"I guess you'll be using that apron a lot once it's finished," he said.

I shook my head. "I'll probably just throw it out," I replied. "We have better aprons at home. Real, store-bought ones."

"Fair enough," he said. Then he sighed. "You know, this is nice, sitting, relaxing here. I just came from your radio station, where I had to shake hands with some poor kid. I thought she was going to wet her pants. And for what?"

I said a quick prayer of thanks that I hadn't won. Also that I wasn't wetting my pants. "A lot of kids really look up to you," I said, staring at my needle and thread. It was easier carrying on a conversation if I didn't have to look at him. "You're their idol. Just like my mother."

"Your mother is an idol?" Ross asked.

"Don't be silly," I said. I said, Don't be silly, to Ross Perlman. "Her idol is Marlon Brando."

"He's great," Ross Perlman said. "I've always wanted to meet him."

At least I tried. "You never have?" I asked.

"We go to different parties," he said. "Does your father have an idol?"

This was not the time to tell a fellow Dartmouth man about Debbie Reynolds. "Laurence Olivier," I said. It seemed to me Dad thought he was a great actor.

"Oh yeah, Olivier," he said. "Your parents have great taste. Tell me, who's your idol?"

"My mom and dad," I said, only I giggled when I said it. Ross burst out laughing. "And you," I admitted, sewing furiously. I prayed he couldn't see how red I was.

"You watch *Joyride?*" he asked.

"Every week," I said. "My brother and mom watch it, too. My father hates it. He grunts every time he sees you."

"Oh, I'm sorry to hear that," Ross said. "I guess you can't please them all."

"He saw you in the TV movie you did, though," I said. "The one about the social worker, and he thought you were very good in that. Really."

"Thank you," he said. "I liked that part a lot."

"I don't blame you," I said. "I mean, I thought it was a good part, too."

"Maybe you could become a critic when you grow up," he said. "It's always good to have one or two in my camp."

"I am thinking about working on a newspaper," I said. "My father does. I guess I could be a critic."

"I'll look for your byline in about ten years," he said. "Except I don't know your name."

"Tracy," I said. "Tracy Newfield."

"Nice name," he said. "It sounds like a critic."

I sat up just a little straighter.

"I always wanted to be an actor," Ross said. "From the time I was born, I think. I really love what I'm doing, but sometimes I think I should have given myself a chance to try something else."

"You sing," I said.

"Yeah, but that's just another type of performing. I mean, something completely different."

"Like physics," I said.

He laughed again. That was three whole times.

"Good point," he said. "I guess I'm doing what I'm good at doing."

"I think you are," I said.

"Thank you," he said. "That means a great deal, coming from a budding critic."

"Oh no!" I cried.

"What is it?" he asked and he jumped from his chair. "Did you stab yourself again?"

"No," I said. "I finished the apron."

Ross laughed again. "It's all for the best," he said. "It is getting pretty late."

I looked at my watch. "You're right," I said. "And I never even called my parents to tell them I wouldn't be home after school."

"Then you'd better call them right now," he said. "Do you have a dime?"

I looked through my wallet. There was a perfectly fine dime in my change purse. "No," I lied.

Ross searched through his pockets. "Here," he said, and tossed it to me.

I felt guilty. "It's okay," I said. "Andrea — she's my best friend — she knew I was going to be here, and she probably called my parents for me. She does things like that."

"She sounds very nice," Ross said. "But call your folks, anyway. Just in case."

"Okay," I said, but I knew I'd never use that

dime. I wondered if I could have a hole drilled in it, so I could wear it as a necklace. I got up and put the apron on Miss Collins' desk.

Ross stood up, too. "It's been nice talking with you, Tracy," he said.

"Thank you," I said. "Good luck tonight."

"You'll be there?" he asked.

"Oh yeah," I said. "Of course."

"I'll be looking for you, then," he said. "Take care."

"You, too," I said, and floated out of there. I put the precious dime in my front pocket, and took one of the ordinary ones out of my change purse and called Mom. I was almost right. Andrea had run into Scott, and he'd called Mom for me. I thought about telling Mom about Ross Perlman, but it was still too incredible for me to get the words out. So we talked instead about what I'd do about supper. She said she'd send a sandwich to me by way of Scott. I didn't think I'd ever want to eat again, so it didn't matter to me.

I sat outside the school for a while, going over the conversation word by word so I'd be able to tell Andrea everything. I realized I should have asked Ross for an autograph for her. I didn't need one — I had my dime and my memories — but Andrea had nothing. I thought about going back to the home ec room to ask Ross for one, but I knew I shouldn't. He was tired and needed to rest. Besides, I didn't want him to think of me as just another pesty kid. If worse came to worst, I'd give Andrea the dime, and just be satisfied with memories and the Band Aid.

"There you are," Scott said, holding a brown paper bag. "Here, this is for you. Now I've got to get my date."

"Thanks, Scott," I said dreamily.

"Hey, Andrea told me about the apron," he said. "I'm sorry. I thought it was a good idea."

"It was a great idea," I said. "It worked out just fine."

He looked at me like I was crazy. "I'll see you after the concert," he said. "Have a good time."

"You, too," I said, and watched as he ran off. He really looked very good.

Something about holding food in my hands made me hungry. I devoured the sandwich and apple Mom had packed. I put the bag in the garbage can, just the way Ross would have, and sat down again, waiting for Andrea. But then it got cool, so I went inside. I'd find everybody there.

"Did you finish the apron?" Andrea asked, as soon as we spotted each other.

"I did," I said. "And I met him. I met Ross."

"You did?" Andrea said. "Really?"

"Really," I said. "He was wonderful."

"Did you get his autograph for me?" she asked. "For my scrap — for my new scrapbook?"

"No, I forgot," I said. "Andrea, I'm really sorry. We just got to talking."

Andrea gave me a funny look. "I think too much sewing has gotten to you," she said. "Let's go in the auditorium."

So we did, and we found our seats. Caroline and Mary Kate were already there. They both looked miserable.

"What's the matter?" I asked.

"No party," Mary Kate said. Caroline looked like she'd never stop pouting. "Ross has to catch a late plane out, so they canceled the party."

I tried very hard to look sad.

"That's terrible," Andrea said, but I could see she wanted to laugh, too.

"There you are," Miss Collins said. She was charging down the aisle, holding something yellow in her hand.

"What is it?" I asked. Caroline looked mean and interested.

"The apron looks decent enough," she said. "For you at least. But really, Tracy, whatever possessed you to write all over it?"

"I didn't write anything," I said. "What are you talking about?"

"This is what I'm talking about," she said, and

held the apron up so she could read it. " 'To Tracy Newfield — future critic and seamstress. Thanks for a lovely talk. Ross Perlman.' "

"He didn't," I gasped.

"I'm sure he didn't," Miss Collins said. "And what I want to know is why you did."

"I didn't," I said. "I mean, he did. Honestly. He was in the home ec room and we talked for a while. He never would have signed it if he'd known it would get me in trouble. Honestly."

Miss Collins sighed. "This Ross Perlman business has gone a little too far," she said. "Now you're hallucinating."

"I am not," I said, but what proof did I have except the apron, which she didn't believe, and a dime with Ross's fingerprints on it? "Really. He was there. We talked. You can ask him."

"I certainly will not," Miss Collins said. "All right, Tracy, we'll talk about this on Monday." And she stormed down the aisle a few more rows and sat down.

"So you've finally gone crazy," Caroline said, and she looked really happy about it. "I knew it had to happen sooner or later."

"She is not crazy," Andrea said. "She did meet him. She told me."

"And you believed her?" Caroline asked. "You're as crazy as she is."

"Thanks, Andrea," I whispered to her. I just wished I'd gotten a real autograph. Not that anybody seemed to believe the one on the apron.

"It's okay," Andrea said. "If you said you talked to him, then you probably did."

I couldn't ask for better. Still, I was glad when the lights went down. First Mr. Thomas came out and told us all about hemophilia. Then the principal came and he introduced Ross to everyone.

And then, there was Ross. He was all dressed up, and he looked different than he had in the home ec room. Sharper, flashier. Maybe not quite as nice.

It didn't matter, though. We were all on our feet shrieking, Caroline as loud as the rest of us.

Ross sang a lot of songs from his *Perlman's Pearls* album. Sometimes it was hard to hear him because of the shrieking. Then he waved us all to sit down.

"I'd like to sing you a new song," he said. "It's called 'Just By Chance,' and it's going to be on my new album, *Green Streets and Gray Fields*."

We all shrieked.

"It's a song about unexpected meetings," he said, ignoring our shrieks. "And I'd like to dedicate it to a girl I met just by chance today, a girl named Tracy Newfield. Tracy, I know you're out there somewhere."

You wouldn't have believed the shrieks then. Everybody stared at me. I thought Caroline would drop dead right at my feet. If I didn't beat her to it.

"Hope you don't mind what I did to your apron," Ross said to me. To *me*. "And I hope Andrea called your folks for you."

"You told him about me," Andrea cried. "Oh, Tracy!"

"So this is for Tracy," he said. "And those just-by-chance meetings." And then he sang his song.

He'll never get a bad review from me.

About the Author

SUSAN BETH PFEFFER is a native New Yorker. She enjoys Emily Brontë, baseball, and film (not necessarily in that order), and has traveled to Tanzania. She graduated from New York University with a B.A. in Television, Motion Pictures, and Radio. She has written many books for young readers and young adults, including *Starting With Melodie*, *Kid Power*, and *Truth or Dare*, available as Apple paperbacks.